Roses
AMIDST THE THORN

THE PARCHED GARDEN

SIMONE C. WILSON

Copyright © 2025 Simone C. Wilson.

All rights reserved. No part of this book may be reproduced, stored, or transmitted by any means—whether auditory, graphic, mechanical, or electronic—without written permission of both publisher and author, except in the case of brief excerpts used in critical articles and reviews. Unauthorized reproduction of any part of this work is illegal and is punishable by law.

ISBN: 979-8-89419-698-5 (sc)
ISBN: 979-8-89419-699-2 (hc)
ISBN: 979-8-89419-700-5 (e)

Because of the dynamic nature of the Internet, any web addresses or links contained in this book may have changed since publication and may no longer be valid. The views expressed in this work are solely those of the author and do not necessarily reflect the views of the publisher, and the publisher hereby disclaims any responsibility for them.

One Galleria Blvd., Suite 1900, Metairie, LA 70001
(504) 702-6708

Contents

The Parched Garden	1
God's Gift	3
Soul Mates	4
Through It All	5
And The Two Shall Be One	7
The Discarded Gift	8
Recognition	9
Specks	10
Contemplations	11
What's Wrong?	12
Bothering Me	14
Walking Away	15
Time Passes	16
I Still Look For You	17
Be Still Accept the Death	18
Finding Truth	19
Always There	20
The Ring	22
Living With Out You	23
Remembering	24
Trying To Understand	25
Guarded Heart	26
Appearances	27
Stolen Glances	28
Change Of Heart	29

Walking In the Spirit..30
I Saw You..31
Coping..32
Judgment 33
Extending the Hand of Forgiveness.................................34
Finding Strength 35
The One That Held My Heart..36
Walk With Me...37
Restoration 38
Giving Up...39
Realization..40
Transformation...41

I thank God for surrounding me with friends and family who encouraged me to write about this life journey.

Merill Alston for reading and suggesting that I share my poetry I had written with others.

A special thanks to my sister Yvonne Mitchell for accompanying me on this difficult life's lesson and encouraged me to keep moving forward.

To my parents Simon& Beatrice Mitchell who through their example demonstrated what truly a loving sustained marriage should reflect.

"The Parched Garden" continues the couple's progression after "Roses Amidst the Thorn". In Roses, we experience the birth, the spiritual co-existence and the unforeseen crumbling of the couple's relationship. The couple finds themselves in a season of dryness. They now live in the wilderness of a broken relationship. They experience a place within themselves where they find no reprieve or solace.

They don't understand what has happened and why God seems to have not helped them find answers to their questions. Though the separation has come, there exist a spiritual connection which continues to bind the couple. They are very much aware of the hurt and pride keeping them from reaching out to each other. Instead of forming a mutual bridge of communication, they begin to search within themselves looking for understanding and insight.

They search for what has brought them to this place. They try to make sense of the devastation left behind; to understand the indifference of their families and close friends, to judge whether their shaken foundation is beyond repair. Finally, to grasp some insight that allows them to know that they will come through their experience.

Knowing within themselves that forgiveness and reconciliation are possibilities the couple must endure the winter season of their relationship. At its end, they will either continue as a couple or part as individuals who have grown from this ordeal.

In God's silence towards them, He still draws them closer to Him. He brings them closer to "The Living Water" that can only quench the thirst of those who have dwelled in this spiritual wilderness.

For in this wilderness, water is available to any who choose to dig deep enough!

"The Parched Garden" is the internal spiritual struggle to keep digging for "The Healing Living Water", so that we learn to nourish the spiritual gardens inside ourselves. We must learn to love ourselves as much as our heavenly Father loves us. Thereby allowing us to extend that love and forgiveness unconditionally to others!

Lark

The Parched Garden

Once our marriage was
A luscious overgrown garden,
Every corner filled with colorful blossoms
And the scent of freshness filled the air

Tending it was easy.
One simply let it go its way
It began spreading green and tiny buds everywhere.
Heaven loved this garden
It showered the necessary moisture
Needed to keep it lush and green.

Many came to the garden,
And because of its abundance
Often they left with enormous bouquets.
The garden didn't worry
About its blossoms were being stolen away.
For it saw the joy it bought to others
So, the garden was contented.
Renewing itself had been so easy.
Involuntary . . . like breathing.

But a fungus started to grow
At first it was so small it was insignificant.
Slowly it became massive
And its thirst was unquenchable.
Every chance it got it drank the clear water
That had fallen to the garden floor.

Soon the garden became parched and brown.
The very earth which fed it became dry and dusty.
Not even the tears wept by the garden
Remembering its beauty could sustain it.

They didn't even try to bring healing waters
Back to replenish the garden.
They accepted its death
And chose to remember
That once there had been
A beautiful lush overgrown garden!

God's Gift

With his infinite knowing
God issues forth
His love to his creations in numerous ways.
The most sacred of these gifts is marriage.
For God's gift to man is his wife.
That he may love, nurture, guide, inspire
And protect her.
His gift to woman is man.
That she may love respect, cultivate
And enlighten the world by sustaining a loving family.

A true appreciation of God's gift
Come when we offer it back to him.
For as we love each other,
We see the face of God.
In His wisdom,
He allows us to explore our divinity by serving
him through our marriage.
For in our marriage we should reflect
God's unselfish and unconditional love.

Remembering to ask God to direct our lives,
His answer will always be
To shine a bright light
On the things we need to see.
Some of these things may be painful
But when we view them
Through spiritual eyes,
The amount of growth,
In love and forgiveness we experience
Unlocks the doors to miracles!

Soul Mates

You and I
Were soul mates
At the world's creation
We had chosen life's path together.

No wonder we felt
So lost, lonely and incomplete
When unresolved issues force us apart
And any separation
Left us diminished.

When we were together,
It was then we felt,
That sense of completeness
We were at peace.
The silence between us
We once thought was void,
Was an expression of the tranquility between us.
And we understood
We can never lose each other.

Through It All

Through every adversity,
You were always the first to put it to prayer.
You gave it to God immediately.
While I quickly lost hope,
I questioned God's plan for us.

I've never heard you challenge our setbacks.
You always made me feel
As if you had a personal conversation with God.
While in that commune,
He shared with you the outcome.

God doesn't close a window, without opening a door.
That spiritual message came from you
With the simple statement
"You gotta believe!"
The spiritual calm which emanated from you
made every situation bearable.

Through our younger relationship
You were the rock, my spiritual example.
You led me down the path
Of rediscovering the faith
That lied dormant within me.

Had our relationship
Not reached this point of breakdown.
I would have never begun searching for God's love
and inner peace within myself.

Through it all
Even when our separation became inevitable
You helped me learn a great lesson.
That God dwells in each of us because we are His creations,
When we call on Him He will always be there.

And The Two Shall Be One

*The interweaving of you and I, began the progression
of two kindred spirits.
Of all the billions of people
Our souls reached out for each other.*

*You were not afraid to hear my soul song.
And I sang it for you
I replenished your inner being with the essence of life.*

*We touched each other's hearts.
We kissed and breathed the breath of oneness into our bodies.
Your thoughts were carefully woven in to my thoughts.
My hurts became your hurts.
And any joy which touched us
Reverberated through each of us
As a single shot of lightning*

*The vessel was forged.
It was hewed from the ethereal mould of God.
We were strong, singleness in consciousness and
trembling with power
That should not have been easily broken!*

The Discarded Gift

Sometimes
God sends a special person,
One who can see our projected image
And still love us in spite of it.

For they look deeper into our persona.
They see God's light within us still glowing.
Knowing just by gazing into our eyes
What we can truly become.
We can receive the love of God that is in our heart.
Despite the darkness we've enclosed it.

Countless times this person
They experience our rages, indifference and cruelty.
Yet, they cling to us
They express words of encouragement and unconditional love.

Our fears, hurts and pain
Often don't allow us to fully hear or become influenced by them.
We may thoughtlessly push them aside
Only to regretfully realize,
What a tremendous gift
We've discarded.

Recognition

I hardly recognized this man standing before me.
There are faint resemblances
Of the person who was a part of me.
I see them lingering around the edges.
But the interior is dark and unfamiliar.
There is a coldness which has settled in your eyes.
A coldness which keeps me separated from you.

Everyday, I ask myself
How did we become strangers?
Was I wrong about what I saw in your face, felt in your touch,
and bonded with your soul.
Could all my senses be so deceived?

But our children
Still see the man they love
And call Daddy.
They look beyond the darkness and coldness
They see your celestial radiance,
And they know you!

Specks

I'm trying to see you as it was in the beginning!
When we had our first encounter
Our eyes met . . .
And even though we came from two different backgrounds,
There was this instant recognition, that we were so much alike.
We only had to take a chance to walk across the bridge.
Facing each other, we walked, embraced and became one.

We seem to be back on that bridge now.
But new elements accompany us
Fear, pride, and distrust cling to our shaken bodies.
We can't see each other clearly for our vision is clouded by them.
But we feel the presence of the other strongly calling to us.
It beckoning us to cross the bridge once more.

I remember all the qualities in you
That over shine all the things my mind projected
as undesirable specks.
However, new found spiritual wisdom allows us to clearly see
The specks we see in each other are reflections of ourselves.
Only healing powers of recognizing God's love within each of us
Can guide us across that bridge,
And restore ourselves as someone who has come
out of the wilderness.

Are we willing to walk through the mist?
Pluck out the specks.
Then cleansed of all guilt and softly brushed with the beauty
Of tiny expressions of forgiveness
We will only see that we have come to
A better understanding of each other

Contemplations

*I sit and contemplate what drove you away.
What could make a man, walk away from what he had created?*

*You formed all our dreams into realities
Then you smashed them into unrecognizable illusions.
For some reason
The life we had envisioned was not enough for you.*

*But my love won't try to hold you.
I know, I must let go
For I understand
Everything will be all right!*

What's Wrong?

What's wrong about giving up on a person?
When is it right to judge their actions?
Justify your reaction.
Hope to find the road to forgiveness so all may heal.

How can healing take place?
When the mind won't let you forget
The betrayal the hurt, and the separation.
When will the incident no longer have any meaning.
Only the restoration of communication becomes important.

What's wrong about protecting yourself?
Protection you need from additional pain, and disappointment?
Insulating your emotions by allowing yourself
To just shut down become numb.

Wrongness lies
In our own thinking
That we can judge others, or decide what is God's plan for us.

Realization must come
That people and situations
Enter into our lives to stimulate our spiritual growth.

We can not numb ourselves to the world.
For our purpose is to shed

*God's light within us
On everything we do.
We must look to Him for strength in times of tribulation.
For when we seek Him in our hearts with true faith and love*

*He will issue judgments
Release our minds, heal the hurts,
And restore communication
He will transform hearts to express love, faith and forgiveness.*

Bothering Me

What's bothering me
About this phase in our relationship
Is that no one wants to help us
Reach another level of understanding or forgiveness.

Our friends and families
Who cried tears of joy for us
At our wedding twenty years ago
Are completely comfortable watching our marriage crumble away.

I hear words around me
"These things happen", Let go and move on",
"Get a new life" "That Life is over".
Everyone has dug a grave for our marriage.
They have placed it in the ground.
And have covered it up.
Without seeing if the corps
Is really dead!
And we believe them.

Walking Away

I've tried so many times.
I've tried to walk away from our relationships.
I've made countless of list in my mind
On hundreds of sheets of paper
I write reasons why I must let go.

Each time I come to that threshold
I can't open the door.
My head reminds me of scripture
"And the two shall become one"
I see the very words on our wedding invitation.
Then my mind flashes pictures
My body reminds me when this was so.

Confused, I walk away from the door.
I ask God to give me some guidance.
Some inner strength insulted with patience.
Hoping you're having the same difficulty
You can't turn away from that threshold too.

Time Passes

Before you realize

Years have gone by
Without you being here with us.
You glance at me
As if it was only yesterday
You decided to walk away.

The children and I know
The years, months, days,
Hours, minutes, and seconds
We know when we were last a whole family.

You seem unaffected by time.
As if when you walked away
Time froze for you.
Somehow, you have become totally numb to your surroundings.

You radiate joy when you're around us.
But as time draws near your departure
Your eyes dim, seeping into darkness.
They are void of the life
Which only moments ago existed there.
Your visits are fewer now.
When we do come together
There is a surge of warmth which defrosts the wall of ice
You've constructed for yourself and us
And time passes.

I Still Look For You

I still look for you, at the end of a busy day.
You're large warm hands massaging my feet.
And I rest my head on my favorite spot upon your shoulder.
Hearing the perfect rhythm of your heart,
I hear your deep voice recalling your day.

I still look for you, in the morning.
Touching your cold empty spot of our bed,
Remembering when the phone would ring,
And with your soothing voice,
You gave to us our morning wake-up-call.
Always seasoned with caring remarks,
Sending us off to school and work,
Knowing we were loved and needed.

I still look for you, on holidays.
Expecting you to burst through the door
You're coming with cards, flowers and unnecessary toys.
Accompanied with your wide smiles,
You come to us with gentle kisses and warm caresses.

I still look for you to share in my life.
Feel the warmth of your presence.
I still look for you!
I still look for you!
Look for you!
Look for you!
For you!
You!

Be Still Accept the Death

Be still, accept the death
The two made one now separated
And the once joined corps lies ready for the autopsy.

No longing or crying can revive its stillness.
Be still, accept the death.
Forget its warmth,
Forget its light, and its familiar happiness.
Remember only its body lies cold, in its pronounced death.
Be still, accept the death.

Mourn its passing.
Grieve its premature death.
Leave the remains, untouched, unquestioned, unresolved
Be still, accept the death.
Accept the death
Be still.

Finding Truth

*Go if you must
But remember
You carry with you our love.
Because we love you we choose
Not to smother you
By letting you seek
What you feel 'You have missed or lost.*

*Remember
In your absence
We are also searching.
For new identities. understandings
And ways of coping
With the void your leaving has created.*

*As God directs our steps
May truth be found by us.
Trusting in God to know
How to fix all circumstances
To his glory and for our happiness!*

Always There

We always manage somehow always there for each other.
There was this mystical umbilical cord which joined us.
It allowed us to feel each others pains and joys.

In our darkest moments,
Shadow with fear and uncertainty
We were always there
Caring, loving and supporting each other
We raised our voices together in prayer.

We took for granted
We would always be there for each other.
Nothing prepared us for the possibility
That we might not be able
To reach out and feel the security of each others support.

Now, that separation has come,
I feel the vast emptiness
Your leaving has created.
At first I thought my life had ended.
For how could I exist without the other part of me?

For a longtime
I wallowed in this pit of low self-esteem and self pity.
I needed time
To cry, feel the hurt, betrayal and anger
Attempt forgiveness and try to heal.

Healing isn't easy.
It's a continuing process engages in daily.
But you know through faith and trust in God
You'll be all right.

There are days
When I question my decision
To let go, and leave you in God's care,
But as I take a closer look
How far I've come in faith and strength
I'm reassured this was God's plan for me.
Even though we are not together
We know we will always
Be there for each other.

The Ring

Why do you still wear our wedding ring?
You have removed yourself
From our lives and reduced our communication to a beeper number

Maybe it has become a prop
For the new scenes you play
Or just another cruel way to hurt me,
saying that your choice is elsewhere.

Our rings are symbol
It is our living covenant with God to love one another.

How can you hold on to a piece of us
And talk of new life with someone else?
While you still wear
A remembrance of our commitment on your hand.

Living With Out You

Suddenly I realize that you are really gone.
The space beside me is empty and cold,
And the fragrance of your cologne
Has long evaporated from your pillow.

Slipping into lonely bed sheets
Now void of the warmth you brought there
I turn to lay my head upon a chest
That's no longer there and won't be returning.

I scan our bedroom only to find
No remembrance of you is visible anywhere.
It's as if you were a lovely dream I once dreamt
Presently gone from my existence,
It is gone from my sight my touch and my love.
But still it is ever present in my conscience.

Remembering

*My nights are lonely now.
I'm remembering your sleeping next to me,
I'm remembering my head gently resting on your shoulder.*

*I'm remembering late night talks.
Conversations about work, kids, the "Eleven O'clock News",
Or just asking did you remember to lock the patio doors.*

*Remembering how we decided
Your working nights would be better financially.
But it helped us to become strangers
We were passing by each other living two separate lives.*

*I had hoped you' were remembering too!
I hoped you were feeling as lonely as me.
Turning to look at your empty space,
I cradle your pillow in my arms.
I smell the scent of you
Catching my tears and trying to remember
Why we thought it was a great decision!*

Trying To Understand

I sit here in the night stillness,
Trying to understand you
Trying to formulate a vision
I try to understand your thoughts, motivations, and actions.
I try not to hurt so badly because our feelings weren't mutual.
Trying to understand . . .
Why my heart still has a place for you
And I whisper to myself,
"Even though you've separated from me
You are still a part of my life!"

Guarded Heart

Carefully I guarded my heart
From people who didn't
Appreciate the innocent
Love offered them.

The caring and understanding,
I thought would materialize in relationships
brought regret and humiliation.
So, I promised myself
I would never open myself completely.
Keeping a part of me always hidden
I safely buried it deep within protected doors.

You were a light that touched my life,
An illumination so great you were able to
Force open the locked doors
There were no visible hints of betrayal.
And I embraced you wholeheartedly.
For your light became my protector.

Slipping in undetected,
Your deceptions came cloaked in carefully planned lies.
Lies, which ate away trust and understanding
My heart, became a mere shadow

Now, only God can create a new heart in me.
Only God can restore His creation
And place me back on the path
Where healing and wholeness
Wait to embrace me.

Appearances

Outward appearances can easily be manufactured.
Surface projections can be anything we wish,
People are easily persuaded
They accept the vibrant images before them.

Very few stop to look beneath the covering.
They are guarding their own secrets,
They flash their own mask.

Taking a closer deeper look
May disclose for the looker
Something they don't wish to see.
Having clearer knowledge causes inevitable change.
Change for the viewer as well as the one being gazed upon.

Somehow we must find
The courage within ourselves
To search for that inner place
It is a place where we can see people with our ethereal eyes.

Focusing on the glorious creation
God formed them to be
Not the manufactured projections
They want us to perceive.

Stolen Glances

I feel you even before you enter the room.
A familiar calm with flickers of excitement
It announces your arrival to every cell of my skin.
Each nerve is tingling with knowledge he is near.

My eyes search to catch a small peek.
My brain instructs me to be cold and distant.
For unspoken desires
May not be reciprocate
Elevated emotions nestled within
Allow me to take a chance to gaze into your eyes.
Feeling rekindled warmth
I quickly turn away
Before you are aware
How much I still love you.

Change Of Heart

Remember how upset I was
While you chose to be with another,
You wore our wedding ring.
The symbol of promises made to each other.
It was our outward declaration of Love and commitment.

How I wanted you to remove it from your finger.
For it no longer held
Your love or pledge to me.

Secretly,
I'd hoped
You'd never take it off.
For I hoped it would remind you of why we chose each other.

I wasn't prepared for this feeling of emptiness.
I saw your abandoned finger.
That sinking feeling overwhelmed me
I'd lost you
And now,
Letting go completely
Is a reality.

Walking In the Spirit

I can walk in the spirit by changing my thoughts.
I can read the word.
I can allow Christ to take dominion over my life.

I now realize my talents.
I know that God has made me gifted.
I can allow myself to share these gifts with loved ones and the world.

Bringing His Love
To those around me
Helping to surface the good
I see in others
Assisting in their healing
As they reach towards
His out stretched arms.

By building a new spiritual bridge
Between my savior and I
Acknowledging his never ending love
I allow Him to lead me to higher awakenings

I Saw You

I saw you standing there
You were trying to evade my eye contact.
You made general conversation.

It's still very uncomfortable.
We both wear our hurts on the inside.
Pretending on the outside
That everything is fine . . . .

We possess the cowardice
To deceive each other
But lack the courage
To say what is needed
I forgive you!

Coping

Myself-esteem is so low

At times I feel that coping with reality is beyond my reach.

I stretch my hands outward
Towards the realities of life
Through the film is my reality . . .
A reality filled with ugliness, insecurity, envy, solitude and darkness.

Yet off in the far distance a simmering glow.
I walk hurried toward the glow
But with every step the glow seems to move further away.

I run . . .
Thinking I must hurry my pace.
I try to catch the simmering glow.
It dodges and weaves.
It continues to evade my reach
And I continue to chase.

Judgment

I could see so plainly all your shortcomings.
You did
That would change me
Into a self-righteous voyeur

I have pass judgments on all your actions and reactions.
Listening ever so carefully with perfect ears
I try to catch any untruth or betrayal.

Time passed
The road to reconciliation seemed barred.
That road was closed until introspection's debut.

Discovery was blinding.
The tunnel vision I had created seemed to widen.
And the very things
I saw disturbing in you
I found boldly manifested in me.

Perhaps, that road of reconciliation was never traveled
Because, of too many detours involving judgments.

It kept us from looking beyond blame.
It kept us from reaching out toward each other
with love and forgiveness.
It kept us painfully apart.

Extending the Hand of Forgiveness

More than anything
I want to move on into a level of mutual forgiveness.
I'm tried of replaying those old hurts, betrayals and painful memories
My prayers are full of longings of release
I pray for release from this relentless dwelling in the past.

Although I am petrified,
My need for peace and joy are greater than fearing loneliness.
So I extend my hand,
Hoping you will reach to clasp it
And by touching unveil the power of healing through
mutual forgiveness.

Finding Strength

Letting go of you wasn't easy.
I wanted to wrap you up
In my protective warmth
Until you realized the path
You had taken was wrong.

But I realized,
There are no wrong paths
Just life experiences
That we must encounter.
Discourses we must learn.
Protection doesn't stop them
Only delay their coming.

So with great reluctance
I opened my arms,
Tried to clear my mind,
And begged my heart
To continue beating,
I placed my fears away.
Understanding,
That God only sends what we can endure
And He won't let me undertake this alone.

The One That Held My Heart

I have always told you that you are the one who held my heart.
We have chosen different directions to follow
But no matter where I am
I will always carry you with me.
From the moment you entered into my life,
I knew I would always need you beside me.

You bring a feeling of calm to me whenever you are near.
Merely the thought of you sends messages of tranquility.
You were the one that inspired my heart
So I reached beyond my expectations.
There is nothing you wouldn't do or attempt for me.

God has given me the strength to trust what has come.
Even though it meant letting you go
What we have shared together will always be there
Never fading, never aging, ever present in my heart!

Walk With Me

Walk with me in a place of beauty.
Where we could,
Finally talk about everything together.

A place where its radiance
Would inspire us
To speak what's truly in our hearts.
Sitting close to you, and gazing deeply into your eyes.
I would open up
And share my deepest desires.

I would leave behind,
All the misunderstandings, foolish pride
I would leave, all the built up walls of unnecessary protection.
Letting our hearts express to truth.

Restoration

Broken and discarded
By all that once beheld its loveliness
Thrown aside, labeled unusable
Not quite as perfect as once regarded.
Yet if viewed closely,
It's essence is still unblemished

God,
With His unconditional love
Gently reaches down,
Gathers up the fragments
Patiently forming them,
Not into the same creation
But something new
And more wonderful
Than the original!

Giving Up

I'm giving up!

Years have passed.
No restoration has occurred
And you appear to be satisfied with this arrangement.

All my hopes of reconciliation are old and worn.
They were ragged intentions
Which were never recognized or shared.

I held on too long.
Now I see some of life's opportunities for happiness
have passed me by.

So, here I am!
I am ready to embrace my freedom.
I commence sweeping remembrance of the past away
I walk towards a new awaiting future.

Realization

I've come to realize . . .
I need never fear losing you.
For you and I will always be one.
We were created from that oneness
And no place, situation or person
Can ever separate you from me.
I will always feel . . .
Your presence with me and you will feel mine.
For we are a part of a greater oneness
That someday we both will return.
So, I am never without you.
For wherever you go I am there.
We are still experiencing this life together!
For as children of God
We know we will return to Him!

Transformation

*In my discovery of a new me
Suddenly I realized ...
who I could and wanted to be.*

*The garden I once was,
No longer parched,
Dried up ...
But ready to receive new fertilized soil,
Growing a more vibrant spectacular garden was the mission.*

*Knowing full well the beauty of its buds and fragrance would bring
new seedlings filled with lessons and renewed faith.
Now, fully implanted in rejuvenated soil.
Filled with self-discovery, self-worth, confidence,
But mostly the importance of self-love.*

*Created a blossom that I had forgotten,
Now bloomed into a radiant rose.
So pungent in love for itself and others,
It glowed in the warmth of the sun.
Strong and stretching to reach the sky!*